THE AMAZING STARDUST FRIENDS

BE A STAR!

By Heather Alexander

Illustrated by Diane Le Feyer

BRANCHES™

SCHOLASTIC INC.

READ ALL ABOUT
THE AMAZING
STARDUST
FRIENDS

THE AMAZING STARDUST FRIENDS
STEP INTO THE SPOTLIGHT!
SCHOLASTIC   HEATHER ALEXANDER
1

THE AMAZING STARDUST FRIENDS
BE A STAR!
SCHOLASTIC   HEATHER ALEXANDER
2

☆ TABLE OF CONTENTS ☆

To Joe, with love — H.A.

To Mum and Dad, who made it all possible — D.L.

Copyright © 2015 by Heather Alexander, L.L.C.
Interior illustrations copyright © 2015 by Scholastic, Inc.

All rights reserved. Published by Scholastic Inc.
Publishers since 1920. SCHOLASTIC, BRANCHES, and associated logos are trademarks and/or registered trademarks of Scholastic Inc.

The publisher does not have any control over and does not assume any responsibility for author or third-party websites or their content.

No part of this publication may be reproduced, stored in a retrieval system, or transmitted in any form or by any means, electronic, mechanical, photocopying, recording, or otherwise, without written permission of the publisher. For information regarding permission, write to Scholastic Inc., Attention: Permissions Department, 557 Broadway, New York, NY 10012.

This book is a work of fiction. Names, characters, places, and incidents are either the product of the author's imagination or are used fictitiously, and any resemblance to actual persons, living or dead, business establishments, events, or locales is entirely coincidental.

Library of Congress Cataloging-in-Publication Data
Alexander, Heather, 1967- author.
Be a star! / by Heather Alexander ; illustrated by Diane Le Feyer.
pages cm. — (The Amazing Stardust Girls ; 2)
Summary: Allie, Bella, Carly, and Marlo, eight-year-old performers in the Stardust Circus, are normally best friends—but when a film crew comes to do a television special on the circus, Allie's dreams of being a Hollywood star threaten to drive a wedge between them.
ISBN 0-545-75754-1 (pbk.) — ISBN 0-545-75755-X (hardcover) — ISBN 0-545-76092-5 (ebook) — ISBN 0-545-76093-3 (eba ebook) 1. Circus performers—Juvenile fiction. 2. Best friends—Juvenile fiction. 3. Ambition—Juvenile fiction. [1. Circus—Fiction. 2. Best friends—Fiction. 3. Friendship—Fiction. 4. Ambition—Fiction.] I. Le Feyer, Diane, illustrator. II. Title.
PZ7.A37717Be 2015
[Fic]—dc23
2014033955
ISBN 978-0-545-75755-3 (hardcover) / ISBN 978-0-545-75754-6 (paperback)

10 9 8 7 6 5 4 3 2   15 16 17 18 19

Printed in China   38
First edition, May 2015
Illustrated by Diane Le Feyer
Book design by David DeWitt
Edited by Katie Carella

The Happy Flip

Dance music blasted in the circus tent. The air smelled of buttered popcorn. The crowd cheered.

I waited backstage. I didn't go out.

Not yet.

I've been in the circus since I was born. I knew to let the crowd's excitement grow.

"It's time for the Stardust Circus parade!" Liam the Ringmaster said into his microphone.

I smiled at my three best friends. We were in the parade together.

"First up is Allie," called Liam. "Allie is the youngest member of the fabulous trapeze family the Flying Faltos!"

The crowd cheered louder.

Then I did back handsprings across the circus tent.

I love to flip.

I can even do a layout somersault on the trapeze. That's a flip in the *sky*!

"Here comes Carly the clown!" Liam told the crowd.

"Beep! Beep!" called my friend Carly Bruni. She zoomed in on a unicycle. Her hot-pink braids stuck out. She held an umbrella and acted like it was raining inside the tent. The crowd laughed. Carly loves making people laugh.

"Hold your horses, folks! It's
Bella, our animal trainer!"
Liam called out.

A white horse galloped in.
My friend Bella Lu stood
on its back. Purple
ribbons in her long,
dark hair flew
behind her.

"Make some noise for Marlo!" cried Liam. "She's new to our parade. She's a hula-hoop whiz!"

Marlo Sommer skipped out. Five colorful hula-hoops spun around her body. Around and around.

Marlo was eight, too—just like Carly, Bella, and me.

The four of us held hands. We kicked our legs high.

"Meet the Amazing Stardust Girls!" called Liam.

My friends *are* amazing!
The spotlight shined on us.

I did a back handspring.

I flip when I'm happy. It's just what I do.

When the show ended, I undid my bun backstage. Mamá makes it so tight and pinch-y! I shook out my thick, brown curls. I pulled on my sparkly hoodie.

"Come on!" I called to my friends.

It was time for my most favorite part of every show: saying hi to my fans. Fans *really* love the circus. They wait outside to meet the performers.

Carly, Bella, Marlo, and I left the tent together. Bella's three white dogs—Marshmallow, Tofu, and Coconut—followed. Bella always has animals with her.

"Amazing Stardust Girls!" yelled a tall girl. "Can I get your autograph?"

"For sure!" I said.

I didn't sign my full name— Alejandra Padillo Falto.

I wrote: *Allie.*

I always dotted my *i* with a star.

"Your turn," I said, handing the girl's paper to Carly. Then I signed another autograph. And another.

All with stars.

"My hand is tired," whispered Bella.

"Not me," I said. "I could sign autographs all night!"

"It's time to go. And I have two *amazing* surprises," said Marlo.

She raced off with Carly and Bella.

I chased after my friends.

Then I did another back handspring for the fans. I just *had* to!

Surprise Number One

Where are you taking us, Marlo?" I cried.

Marlo ran past the long, purple Stardust Circus train. Everyone in the circus lives on the train. Each part of the train is called a *car*. There are apartment cars, a restaurant car, and even a school car. Our train is the coolest place to live. And it drives us from show to show.

↑ HORSES

☆ Bella's Family ☆

↓ MEDIA & GAME CAR

↙ CIRCUS OFFICE

C SAFE

PERFORMERS' APARTMENTS

↓ DRESSING ROOM CAR

☆ Marlo's Family ☆

↑ PIE CAR

↓ PROPS CAR

↑ ACTING CAR

CREW & STAFF ↑

↑ LOCOMOTIVE ENGINE

"Hurry!" Marlo waved us around back.

Bella's guinea pig, Boris, sniffed the air. "Boris smells hamburgers," said Bella.

"Look!" I pointed to tables set up in the field. "Everyone's here."

Acrobats. Clowns. Dancers.

And my big trapeze family: Papi and Mamá sat with my two cousins. My teenage sisters, Renata and Danna, shared a picnic blanket.

"Surprise!" called Marlo. "My mom made a big barbecue!"

12

Marlo's mom is our circus cook.

She makes the *best* food.

Mamá says Marlo's mom's salsa is as good as my *abuela*'s. That's *huge*. My family came from Mexico, and my grandma is famous for her spicy salsa.

And for her triple somersault on the trapeze.

She's that kind of grandma.

We're that kind of family.

I stood in line behind Carly. She piled her plate with cheeseburgers, corn, potato chips, and pickles.

Marlo's eyes widened.

"Clowning makes me hungry," Carly said proudly.

I sat with my friends. Bella fed Boris a potato chip. Carly popped a whole pickle in her mouth.

"Hey, Marlo," I said. "You said there were *two* very amazing surprises. What is Surprise Number Two?"

Marlo's green eyes twinkled. "We're going to have a party—a paint party!" she said.

"I love parties!" I jumped up.

"And I love painting!" said Bella.

"But I'm still eating," said Carly.

I laughed. I knew Carly. She wouldn't budge until she was finished. Even for a party.

Finally, Carly ate her last chip.

We got on the train with everyone else. A whistle sounded. The train began to chug on the tracks.

"We're off to our next show," said Bella.

"And the four of us are off to a fabulous paint party!" I said.

We ran through the train.

3 Surprise Number Two

Bella and Marlo tied their hair back as we hurried into the Pie Car.

The Pie Car is the train's restaurant. It's where Marlo's mom cooks. When Marlo first saw the Pie Car, she said it needed a makeover. Carly's mom sewed pretty lavender tablecloths to decorate it.

Now Marlo's mom handed us each a smock, a brush, and a bucket of paint.

"Time to say good-bye to these ugly olive-green walls," she said.

"With pink paint!" said Carly.

Carly is all about pink.

I'm more of a blue girl.

"Let's paint!" I said. I couldn't wait to start!

"Don't make a mess," warned Marlo's mom, going into the kitchen.

"We need tunes," said Bella. She turned on music.

Then Bella painted hearts. Marlo painted flowers. Carly made swirls.

I painted a big, drippy star, while I did the Twist.

My brush splattered paint on Carly's smock.

"Hey!" Carly laughed. She flicked her brush at me.

"Boris, duck!" cried Bella as paint flew back and forth. Bella always talked to her animals.

"Boris, Boris, you are so smart,
You hide away when we do art."

I giggled. "That's so cute. You made a rhyme for him."

"I'm practicing for our Poem Day at school tomorrow," said Bella. "I wrote my poem about a bunny. But maybe I'll use this new poem."

"Mine's about rainbows," said Marlo.

"Mine's about pizza. And a wizard," said Carly. "I can't wait to share it!"

"What's yours about, Allie?" asked Bella.

I gulped. "I'm still working on it."

Carly rolled her eyes. She knew I forgot the homework. Again.

Luckily, just then Liam opened the door.

"Hello, Stardust Girls!" boomed Liam. "Sorry to crash your fabulous paint party. But I'm walking our guests through to the other cars."

We all stopped painting.

"Meet Teegan and Brett," said Liam. "They're riding with us to Hollywood."

"Hollywood?" I asked. My heart began to beat fast.

"Yes," said Liam. "We'll do two shows there."

"And we'll be filming both shows for a TV special," said Teegan.

"*¡Fabuloso!*" I cried. Our circus was going to be on TV! I got a tingly feeling.

"See you soon," said Brett. He and Teegan left with Liam.

"I'm scared to be on TV," said Marlo. "What if I drop my hula-hoops?"

"Don't worry. I'll run out and make it funny," said Carly. "Do you think I can make the people watching us on TV laugh?"

"For sure," I said. Then I did a happy dance. "Hollywood people are *here*! I *so* want to be a TV star!"

"Wow! Really?" asked Marlo.

"Allie's dreamed about it since we were little," said Carly.

Bella nodded. "And I want Boris to be a TV star, too."

"Boris?" I couldn't hold back my surprise. We all laughed.

"Me and you, Boris." I tickled his furry head. "We'll both be stars."

Boris twitched his nose. He was excited.

But I was more excited.

My dream was finally coming true!

4   Hollywood, Here I Come!

The next morning, I stared out the window. Our train zoomed past a farmhouse.

Across my bedroom, my sisters got ready for school.

All the Flying Faltos live together. Our train car has four bedrooms, a family room, and a small kitchen. My parents are in one bedroom. My aunt and uncle are in another. My cousins are in a third. And I share the fourth bedroom with Danna and Renata.

It is cozy.

It is crazy, too.

"Allie, you're sitting on my favorite shirt!" cried Danna.

"I am not." I chewed on my pencil. "What rhymes with *fly*?"

I was writing my poem.

"Get up!" Danna pulled my arm.

"Mamá!" I yelled.

Mamá hurried into our room. "Girls! Stop bickering!"

"I'm going to be a TV star when we get to Hollywood tomorrow," I told everyone.

"That TV crew is not only here to film *you*, Allie," Danna pointed out.

"Maybe. But once they film me, they won't be able to stop," I said. "I will sparkle for the camera. When I'm famous, I'll change my last name to Sparkle. Allie Sparkle."

"How about Allie Dreamer?" teased Renata.

"Yeah," agreed Danna. "You're definitely living in a dreamworld. That's why you're still in your pj's!"

"Miss Ross will be mad if you're late for school, Allie," said Mamá.

Our teacher, Miss Ross, is a clown. She jokes about everything—except being late.

Danna and Renata left for school. Mamá walked into the family room.

I dressed quickly. I put on my favorite glitter leggings. Then I practiced my star poses in the tall mirror.

Hands on hips. Hair back. Big smile.

I wrote my new name on my paper.

"Hurry, *mi estrella*," said Mamá. That meant *my star* in Spanish!

I tossed my half-finished poem in my bag. I raced down the train's halls. At the School Car door, I peeked inside. The seven other circus kids were already seated.

Miss Ross was teaching. I would enter quietly and take my seat next to Bella.

Then I saw Teegan and Brett.

Brett's camera was on. He filmed Bella, who listened to Miss Ross. Marshmallow, Tofu, and Coconut sat by her feet.

I wanted to be filmed, too.

I looked at the camera. I looked at Miss Ross.

I had an idea.

An idea that could get me into trouble—or make me a star!

My idea was so funny. I *had* to do it. I began to giggle.

I flipped over.

Then I walked into the School Car.

On my hands. Upside down.

Everyone gasped and giggled.

"Show-off," whispered Danna.

"Miss Ross isn't laughing," whispered Marlo.

I didn't stop. I reached my desk and stayed upside down.

Bella smiled. She's seen me walk on my hands a million times.

"That's *so* circus!" cried Teegan. "Brett, are you filming her?"

"I sure am," said Brett. He pointed his camera at me.

Tofu licked my nose.

My arms shook. "Tofu! Your doggie kisses tickle!"

"Alejandra. Up on your *feet*. Now," called Miss Ross.

Uh-oh. I flipped right side up.

"Sorry," I said, quickly taking my seat.

Brett turned his camera to Miss Ross.

"Back to our lesson, class," said Miss Ross. "Our couplet poems have two lines. The last word of each line rhymes. Who wants to share a poem?"

Carly waved her arm. She was super-excited.

But Miss Ross called on Carly's little brother, Leo. He wore a red foam ball on his freckled nose. He read his poem:

"On my clown head
I wear a nose that's red."

Leo grinned. "*Head* and *red* are my rhyming words."

"Nice job!" Miss Ross drew a smiley face next to Leo's name.

"That kid is a great performer," Teegan whispered to Brett.

Just wait, I thought. *An acrobat can outperform a clown!*

Then Danna and Renata read their poems.

"Who's next?" Miss Ross asked when they finished.

Carly raised her hand high.

I wanted to be filmed again. I waved my arm like a windmill.

Miss Ross chose me.

I walked to the front. Suddenly, I felt nervous. My poem wasn't finished.

When Marlo first came to the circus, she was nervous to hula-hoop. "Just add sparkle and wow," Carly had told her.

I would add sparkle and wow to my poem.

I had on my glitter leggings. That was sparkle.

And I leaned into a back bend to add wow.

I peeked my head between my legs.

"I grab the trapeze and fly," I said in a loud voice.

"I sparkle . . ."

I couldn't think of a word to rhyme with *fly*.

Brett was filming. I had to say something . . . do something . . . FAST!

I stood and leaped into a high split! *"Like a TV star!"*

Carly sighed. Marlo raised her eyebrows. Bella frowned.

"Allie, your poem does not rhyme," said Miss Ross.

"I'll write a better poem tonight," I promised.

Miss Ross nodded. Then she put an *X* next to my name.

But I smiled extra big for Brett's camera. Hollywood didn't care about rhymes.

"We will read the rest of the poems another day, class," said Miss Ross. "We have to do math before lunch."

All through math, I stared at my name on the board.

No more Allie, I thought.

Soon, I would be Allie Sparkle!

The pink walls look pretty," said Bella. We were eating lunch together in the Pie Car.

"They sure do!" I bit into a french fry.

"I like all the pink, but how can we make the Pie Car look more circus-y?" Marlo asked.

Carly didn't say anything.

That was weird. Carly was always the first with a sparkly idea.

"What's wrong, Carly?" I asked.

Carly frowned. "I didn't get to share my poem. You took too long, showing off for the Hollywood people."

"I'm sorry," I said. "Do you want to read it to us now?"

"No. I want Miss Ross to hear it first." Carly smiled a little.

Teegan passed our table, holding a stack of photos. "Hi, girls. You were all great in class."

"Did you like my poem?" I asked.

"Seriously?" Carly said under her breath.

But I just *had* to know!

"I did like your poem." Teegan grinned. "The camera really loves you, Allie."

"*¡Gracias!* Thanks!" I cried.

"And when we get to California, I will film all of you in the circus," she said.

I will have to be really good on the trapeze tomorrow, I thought.

"Do you want to eat with us?" asked Bella.

Teegan smiled. "That's sweet, but I have work to do."

"What kind of work?" asked Marlo.

Teegan held up the stack of photos. Each photo had a different girl's face on it. "I need to go through these photos to find a star for my new TV show."

I studied the photo on top. The girl looked like she was my age.

"Teegan!" Brett called from the kitchen. He was filming Marlo's mom.

"Coming." Teegan turned to go.

"Hey, what about me for your new show?" I asked.

"I need you *now*, Teegan!" Brett yelled.

"Fine," Teegan said, heading toward the kitchen.

Had she heard me? I squeezed past Marlo and began to follow Teegan.

"Ask again," whispered Marlo.

"What about *me* for your show?" I asked Teegan again.

"Teegan!" yelled Brett.

"Okay," she called as she hurried away.

Woo-hoo! She said *okay*!

I might be the star of Teegan's new TV show!

Tiny Blue Speck

After lunch, I raced my friends to the Acting Car. Every afternoon, the four Stardust Girls have a special circus class. Sometimes it's dancing, gymnastics, or, like today, acting.

I wondered if the girls in Teegan's pictures were good at acting.

I bet they were.

"Listen up, girls," said Ms. Sarr, our acting teacher. "In the circus, you use your bodies and faces to tell a story. Today we're going to practice acting *without* words."

Ms. Sarr had us sit on the floor, one behind the other.

"Pretend you are on a roller coaster," said Ms. Sarr. "It's going fast. Up and down. Around curves. Ready, set, act!"

In front of me, Carly raised her arms. She leaned to one side. Then the other.

Behind me, Bella grabbed onto my shoulders.

I had never been on a roller coaster. I wasn't sure what to do.

So I swayed back and forth like Carly.

"Show me an excited face," Ms. Sarr told us.

I made my eyes wide.

"Now show me a scared face," she said.

I opened my mouth.

"Excellent, Carly!" cried Ms. Sarr. "Everyone, see how scared Carly looks."

Carly was the best actress of all of us. Acting is a huge part of being a clown.

"Now, come look at your faces in the mirror," said Ms. Sarr.

I looked at my face. The face of Allie Sparkle!

"I might be in a TV show," I blurted out to Ms. Sarr. "Teegan has all these photos of girls, and she's going to look at me, too."

Carly shook her head. "I don't think Teegan really said that."

"I think she did. I heard her," said Bella.

"If she did, Teegan will watch Allie closely at tomorrow's show," said Ms. Sarr.

"I'm ready!" I liked when people watched me perform.

"But it's hard to see Allie way up on the trapeze," said Marlo. "And her family all wears the same blue leotards."

Oh, no! Marlo was right. I would blend in with everyone else. "I'm also the smallest one up there," I said. "I will look like a tiny blue speck."

"Teegan will see your really cool layout somersault," said Bella.

"Yeah, but Renata does a *double* somersault. And my cousin Luis does an even cooler *triple* somersault," I said.

"Back to acting, everyone," said Ms. Sarr.

"Don't worry," Marlo whispered in my ear. "I know how to make you stand out." Then she told me the BEST idea ever!

"What are you guys whispering about?" asked Carly.

I couldn't tell her. Or Bella. Or anyone.

Marlo's idea had to stay a secret until show time—or it wouldn't work.

My lips were zipped!

8 Quick-Change

The next morning, the circus train stopped in California. I watched out my window as the crew set up the big tent by the beach.

I *hate* keeping secrets.

Luckily, I didn't see my friends all day. We had no school on circus days. We were busy practicing. That made keeping my secret a lot easier!

Then it was show time.

"Hi, guys!" I said, finding Carly, Bella, and Marlo backstage. The show was halfway done. I peeked out the curtain. Teegan and Brett sat in the front row. Brett's camera was rolling.

Marlo grabbed my hand. "Come on, Allie," she whispered. "Your family's trapeze act is next. We have to go *now*."

Marlo and I ran to the bathroom.

When we got back, Carly looked at me and then at Marlo. We both wore the same blue-and-white silk robe that my family wears before our act.

"Marlo, why are *you* wearing that robe?" asked Carly, crossing her arms.

"*You* can't be a Flying Falto, Marlo," joked Bella. "You get dizzy in dance class!"

"Allie lent me an extra robe," said Marlo, blushing. Then we shared a secret look.

"What's *really* going on?" asked Carly.

"Here comes the fabulous Flying Falto Family!" Liam called to the crowd.

The band began to play.

My parents, aunt, uncle, cousins, and sisters stood in front of me. They took off their robes. Their blue leotards sparkled.

I slipped off my robe.

Bella gasped. And so did Carly.

"Now I'll stand out," I told them.

I was not dressed in blue.

I was wearing Marlo's rainbow-swirl unitard.

Maybe my new name should be Rainbow Allie! I thought.

Then I ran into the bright lights.

My family climbed the tall ladders to the trapeze platforms. I began to climb, too.

I couldn't wait for Teegan and Brett to see my layout somersault.

My family stared down at me. Their mouths hung open. Mamá and Papi looked angry.

Uh-oh. I was going to be in *big* trouble when I got to the top!

But I couldn't turn back. I had to keep climbing if I wanted to be a star.

9

Rainbow Allie

So much for Rainbow Allie! And forget about anyone seeing my somersault! My parents didn't let me do *anything*.

I ran backstage as soon as our act ended.

"Why didn't you let me do the trapeze?" I asked Mamá.

"Switching costumes was wrong, Allie," said Mamá, "and dangerous."

"I'm used to seeing all blue," said Papi. "It's harder for me to catch you when you're in a different color. You could fall."

"I just wanted to stand out this one time," I said, "because—"

I was going to tell my parents about Hollywood and Teegan, but Liam came over. He looked upset, too.

The Flying Faltos are a *group,* Allie," he said. "You are part of that group. No surprise costume changes."

"I'm sorry," I said. And I meant it.

The band played a drumroll. Liam hurried back out into the ring. Mamá and Papi left to get changed.

I sat on the floor. My family was upset. Liam was angry. I had messed up—big time.

My friends rushed over to me.

"Sorry, Allie. Maybe that was not my best idea," said Marlo.

"I was the one who did it," I said. I didn't blame Marlo.

Carly held out a balloon.

Boom! Carly popped the balloon. Candy poured out!

Bella and Marlo laughed at Carly's clown trick. I ate the sour gummies.

I wanted to go back in time, to have worn my blue leotard. Then I would have done *something* on camera. Not just stand on the platform.

"And now . . . the circus parade!" called out Liam.

"Oh, no! We still need to swap costumes!" cried Marlo.

Dancers and acrobats ran past us.

"There's no time," said Carly. "Keep on Allie's leotard to hula-hoop."

"I can't!" Marlo bit her lip. "Allie's leotard didn't fit me . . ."

"What's under your robe?" asked Bella.

"My underwear!" Marlo turned bright red.

"What?" I cried.

"I can't hula-hoop in my *underwear.*" Marlo looked at me. The parade was starting.

I had to fix this mess—and fast!

10

Dance, Act, Flip

Here come the Amazing Stardust Girls!" called Liam.

The crowd cheered. My heart beat loudly.

I turned to Marlo. "Where's my blue leotard?"

Marlo pulled it from her robe pocket.

I turned to Carly. "Can you keep the crowd laughing while we change?"

"Easy-peasy!" Carly skipped into the tent.

"Hurry!" Bella called to us. She hopped on her horse and rode out.

Marlo and I ducked into a corner. I pulled off her rainbow unitard and tossed it to her. She gave me my blue leotard.

"Quick! Grab your hula-hoops!" I called to Marlo.

We ran into the spotlight.
Whew!

Marlo hula-hooped. I
flipped. Brett filmed the
Amazing Stardust
Girls dancing in
the parade.

"Meet you in the Pie Car!"
I called to my friends after
the show.

Soon, we all squeezed together in a booth. Marlo's mom made us triple-berry smoothies.

Marlo opened her art supplies box. She gave out markers and paper. I doodled.

"The costume switch didn't work the way I planned," I said.

"I didn't know it could be dangerous," said Marlo.

"That's because you're still new to the circus, Marlo," said Carly. "I would have told you, if you had let me in on the big secret."

"I'm sorry, it's just—" I started.

"Allie, you only think about yourself and that Hollywood camera now," said Carly.

"That's not true!" I cried.

"Oh, really?" Carly pointed to my doodles.

Allie Sparkle
Rainbow Allie

"What are those?" asked Bella.

"My TV names," I said.

"Well, Teegan is over there," said Carly. Teegan sat by herself at the counter. "Why don't you *tell* her that you're her big TV star?"

"Maybe that's too pushy," said Bella.

"Yeah, I'm not sure that's a good idea," added Marlo.

Was it a bad *idea?*

Tomorrow was our last show here. Then I would leave Hollywood—and my big chance—behind forever. I couldn't let that happen.

I marched over to Teegan. My friends leaned in to listen.

"Hi, Allie," Teegan said.

So far, so good.

"So . . . did you pick a girl for your new TV show yet?" I asked.

"No, but I'm close to choosing." Teegan smiled. It felt like a secret smile. Just for me.

"I didn't get to do the trapeze tonight," I said quickly. I didn't tell her why. "But I will do it in tomorrow's show."

"I'm excited to see your somersault," she said. "Can you come backstage before the show? To film some footage?"

Footage? A Hollywood word!

"*¡Sí!* Sure!" I cried. "What will you film?"

Teegan shrugged. "You can dance or act or flip," she said.

I went over the list in my head:

"Got it!" I said.

I raced back to my friends. We put our heads together.

"Wow!" said Carly.

"What's *footage*?" whispered Marlo.

"I think it's an audition or tryout," said Bella.

"A *real* tryout!" Carly gave me a surprised smile. "You were right."

I was! I had an audition tomorrow. Up close. *By myself.*

"We could help you practice if you want," said Carly.

"Thanks," I said.

My hands felt sweaty.

I didn't want to tell my friends, but suddenly I was scared.

11

My Show, My Way

I woke up bright and early the next morning.
I rushed to the Dance Car. My friends were
already there, ready to help me.

I practiced a dance for my audition.

"More twirls," said Carly.

"More kicks," said Marlo.

"More leaps," said Bella.

I twirled. I kicked. I leaped.

Bella's three dogs watched on puffy pillows.

"Do you want Marshmallow or Tofu to dance with you?" asked Bella. "Coconut can't help. He always mixes up his left paw and his right paw."

"So do I!" said Marlo.

"Thanks, Bella. But I don't think there are dogs in my TV show," I said.

"It's not yours yet," said Carly.

Why did she say that? I was already nervous.

"But I *really* want it to be." I thought about my audition. "I'm great at flips. I'm pretty good at dancing. But acting . . . well . . ."

"Practice acting something now," said Bella.

I pretended to unwrap a birthday present and find a snake inside.

"Make your scared face more like this," said Carly. She showed me how.

I wished my acting were better.

I tried again.

"I cannot wait until you're a big TV star," said Marlo.

"Me, too," I said. "Then you guys can come visit me in Hollywood."

"Visit you?" said Bella. "You live here on the circus train."

"But TV stars live in Hollywood," I said.

"You can't leave the circus," said Carly. She put her hands on her hips.

"Yes, I can." I hated when Carly acted like a know-it-all. "And I'm going to."

"Really?" Marlo gasped.

I gulped. *There's no way my family would leave the circus to live in Hollywood. Why did I just say that?* I was about to take it back when Carly stomped her foot.

"You can't be a star!" she yelled.

I felt the air go out of me.

"I don't think you should be a star, either," Bella said quietly.

"Me either," added Marlo.

I stared at them: my best friends. They were always there for me.

Until now.

"None of you are on my side?" I asked.

No one said anything.

I blinked back my tears.

"Fine!" I cried. "I don't need you! I'm going to be a star all on my own!"

Then I ran home.

12   Do-over and Over

I wanted to hide under my covers. But my sisters hogged our room, getting ready for our second California show.

Mamá made me sit. She pulled my wild hair into a too-tight bun.

Were my friends all getting ready in the Dressing Room Car?

Without me?

Thinking about them made my tummy flip. In a not-happy way.

I don't need them. I had a show to do. And I had my big audition.

My dad stepped in. "Allie, that Hollywood lady is looking for you," said Papi.

"Can I go now?" I asked.

Papi nodded. "I'll see you backstage."

I ran off to meet Teegan and Brett. They stood outside the tent.

"We'll film here," Teegan said. She pointed to the beach.

I slipped off my shoes. I dug my toes into the warm sand.

"Let's start with dancing," said Teegan. She had on big dark sunglasses.

"Where's the music?" I asked.

"No music," called Brett. "Just dance."

Just dance? Okay. I could do that.

I hummed a song. *Dum-de-de-dum.*

Kick. Leap. Twirl.

On the twirl, a spray of sand flew up. And landed in my mouth!

"Ugh!" I spit out the wet sand.

"Oh, boy," said Brett. "We won't use that."

"Sorry! I can dance better," I said.

"That's okay, Allie," said Teegan. She handed me a paper. "Here. Read this."

Oh, no! I had practiced acting *without* words.

"Hi, I am Allie. I fly with the Flying Fl-Fl-alto Family," I read.

Oops! That was a tongue twister!

"Could I have a do-over?" I asked.

Then I did *six* do-overs!

I *really* wished my friends were here. Carly would make me laugh. Bella would hug me. And Marlo would help me learn these lines.

"How about doing some of your big flips?" asked Teegan.

"Yes!" Flips were my thing.

I looked around. *Why hadn't I practiced on the sand this morning?*

The beach was huge. The ocean was even bigger. I felt small and alone.

I started to flip.

Bam! I landed on my belly. With more sand in my mouth!

Up on the trapeze, my family was there to catch me.

In the parade, my friends were by my side.

I didn't like this strange, lonely feeling.

Is this what being a TV star felt like?

It didn't feel good.

"Thanks, Allie. We're done," said Teegan.

Brett packed up his camera.

My audition was over. *¡Finito!* And I hadn't shown them anything good.

I was so mad. Mad at myself. And mad at my friends for not being here.

My dream had turned into a nightmare.

I would never be a star.

13

Bumping Cones

I ran from the beach into the tent. I ran past the ticket booth. I ran past the cotton candy stand.

"Surprise!" Marlo, Bella, and Carly leaped out at me.

"W-what?" I cried as Carly tossed pink glitter.

"What's going on, girls?" Teegan hurried up behind me.

"It's a going-away party for Allie," said Carly.

"Where's Allie going?" asked Teegan.

"She's moving to Hollywood," said Marlo.

"No. I'm not," I told them. "I messed up my audition."

"What audition?" asked Teegan.

"The footage," I said. "We knew it was *really* an audition to be the star of your new show."

"No . . . that footage was extra bits for the circus special," said Teegan. "I'm filming other performers, too."

"But you had all those photos. And I asked about being in your new TV show," I told her. "You said okay, and then later you asked me about the footage."

My friends all nodded.

"I'm sorry, Allie. That wasn't what I meant," said Teegan.

"So you weren't *ever* thinking of me?" I asked.

Teegan shook her head. "And I picked a girl last night to be the star. I'm sorry."

Then Teegan hurried off.

I glanced at Carly. I waited for her to say, "I told you so."

She didn't.

"So Allie's still a Stardust Girl!" cried Bella.

"Woo-hoo!" called Marlo.

"We didn't want you to leave," said Carly.

Suddenly, I understood. "Is that why you said I couldn't be a star?"

"Well, first I was mad, because you were acting all bigheaded," said Carly. "Then when you said you'd move away, I got sad."

"We didn't want you to be a star," said Marlo. "We'd miss you too much."

"But we talked after you ran off. We weren't being good friends. So we threw this party—to try to make up for that," said Bella.

"We're cool with you being a TV star," said Carly. "If that's what you want."

"I thought I wanted to be a star more than anything. But I was wrong," I said. I remembered that lonely feeling on the beach. "You guys are my best friends. I love being a Stardust Girl. I don't want to stop."

"Ever?" asked Carly.

"Ever," I said.

Bella handed us each a big cone of pink cotton candy.

"Let's bump cones," she said. "It can be our new good-luck thing. Bumping cones won't hurt like bumping noses."

"One . . . two . . . three!" I called.

Splat! We smushed our cones together.

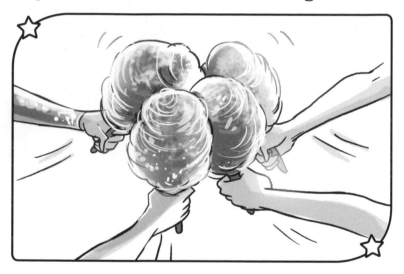

"Oh! It's sticky," said Marlo.

"But yummy!" Carly took a big bite.

"The Stardust Girls stick together!" I grabbed my friends' sticky hands. "Let's go! We have a show to do."

14

Stars!

I didn't think about Brett's camera during the show.

I flipped with my family up on the trapeze. I flipped alongside my friends in the parade.

Happy flips.

After the show, we signed autographs. Lots of them.

Teegan waited by the train to say good-bye.

"May I add your photo to my pile?" she asked me. "In case I need a trapeze girl in a TV show someday."

"Sure!" I did a flip—just for her.

"Allie!" Carly stuck her head out the window. "We're leaving."

"Not without me!" I hurried aboard.

Soon, the train sped away from Hollywood.

I sat with my friends in the Media and Game Car. All the circus people were here. Liam turned off the lights. Teegan and Brett's show came on the big screen.

"There's Boris!" said Bella. Boris peeked out from her pocket as she danced.

"My hula-hoops didn't fall," said Marlo.

"The crowd is laughing!" said Carly.

I was on the screen now. Way up on the trapeze platform. They must have filmed this part at tonight's show.

I grabbed the trapeze bar. Then I flew through the air, right into Papi's strong arms.

Then Mamá flew. Then Danna and Renata.

We all looked amazing in our sparkly blue leotards.

"It's us again!" cried Carly, pointing. On the screen, we all held hands in the parade.

The crowd called our names.

Carly! Bella! Marlo! Allie!

And then it hit me.

I was a star. We all were.

"I have an idea! Follow me," I told my friends.

We ran to the Pie Car. I shared my idea as I pulled shiny gold paper from Marlo's box.

Then Carly traced stars.

Bella cut out the stars.

Marlo wrote a circus performer's name on each star.

I dotted every *i* with a star.

We hung up the sparkly stars.

Marlo looked around. "The Pie Car looks so circus-y. I love it!"

Carly ran to get everyone. Every acrobat. Every clown. Every Flying Falto.

"Ta-da!" we cried, when they all squeezed in.

"There's my name," called Leo, pointing to his star.

"And mine," said Danna.

"That's right," I said. "The Stardust Circus is *filled* with stars."

I pointed to my star: Allie.

"But what about Allie Sparkle and Rainbow Allie?" asked Marlo.

"I like me best as *Allie*," I said.

"Me, too," said Carly.

"Me, three," said Bella.

"Me, four," said Marlo.

"Group hug!" I cried.

I was so happy.

I wanted to flip.

But the Pie Car was too crowded.

Good thing we were on our way to our next show. I would do a lot of flips there—up on the trapeze and beside my friends, the Amazing Stardust Girls!

HEATHER ALEXANDER lives in New Jersey, with her husband, two daughters, and a small white dog, who does very few tricks but is awfully cute.

When she was younger, Heather used to be a figure skater. She still loves everything to do with twirling, jumping, and glitter. Lots and lots of glitter!

Heather is the author of more than forty books for kids. THE AMAZING STARDUST FRIENDS is her first early chapter book series.

DIANE LE FEYER lives in a magical land called France, where there are lots of big castles and very good food. As a child, she was always drawing and dreaming of glitter and sparkle! As an adult, she makes her living drawing fantastical scenes, working in 2-D animation (both as a director and animator), and teaching young artists. She is a teacher, an artist, a bad cook, and a mother. She has a darling daughter, a loving husband, and a goldfish named Bubbles.

THE AMAZING STARDUST FRIENDS

BE A STAR!

✦ QUESTIONS & ACTIVITIES ✦

What is Marlo's secret plan to help Allie stand out in the show? Does the plan work?

Explain the **difference** between what Allie thought Teegan was saying about the TV star role and what Teegan was actually saying.

Reread pages 71-72. What does Allie mean when she says, "Thinking about them made my tummy flip"?

Would you want to be a TV star, a circus star, or a regular kid? Explain.

Write a **couplet poem** like the Stardust Girls do in school. Look back at pages 18 and 31 for examples. And make sure the last word of each line rhymes!